THE SOURCES OF THE STORIES

There are many versions of the fairy tales told
in this book. The storytellers listed below
wrote, or wrote down, the best-known versions,
on which the present tellings are based. The
date is the original year of publication.

The Three Little Pigs · Joseph Jacobs 1890
The Frog Prince · Jacob and Wilhelm Grimm 1812
The Enormous Turnip · Jacob and
Wilhelm Grimm 1812
The Sultan's Daughter was derived from several
Middle Eastern folk-tales.

Copyright © 1985 by Walker Books Ltd.
All rights reserved.
This 1986 edition is published by Derrydale Books, distributed by
Crown Publishers, Inc., 225 Park Avenue South, New York,
New York 10003, by arrangement with Walker Books, Ltd.
Manufactured in Italy
Library of Congress Cataloging in Publication Data
Hayes, Sarah.
The three little pigs.
(Read me a story)
Summary: Retellings of well-known fairy tales from
Jacobs, Grimm, and the Middle East.
1. Fairy tales. [1. Fairy tales. 2. Folklore]
I. Hadley, Colin, ill. II. Title. III. Series: Hayes, Sarah.
Read me a story.
PZ8.H333Th   1986   398.2′4529734   [E]   86-11580
ISBN 0-517-61555-X
h g f e d c b a

THE THREE
LITTLE PIGS

THE FROG PRINCE

THE SULTAN'S DAUGHTER

THE ENORMOUS TURNIP

Retold by Sarah Hayes

Illustrated by Colin Hadley

DERRYDALE BOOKS • NEW YORK

THE THREE LITTLE PIGS

Once there was an old mother pig who had three little pigs. She was too poor to feed them so she sent them off to seek their fortunes.

The first little pig met a man with a load of straw. 'Please, man,' he said, 'will you give me that load of straw?' The man set down the straw and the little pig built himself a fine house with it.

Then along came a wolf. He saw the little pig in his fine house of straw and he knocked on the door. 'Little pig, little pig, let me come in,' he said.

The little pig answered, 'No, no, by the hair of my chinny chin chin, I will not let you in.'

And the wolf replied, 'Then I'll huff and I'll puff and I'll blow your house in.'

So he huffed and he puffed and he blew the house in. Then he ate up the first little pig.

The second little pig met a man with a load of sticks. 'Please, man,' he said, 'will you give me that load of sticks?' The man set down the sticks and the little pig built himself a fine house with them.

Along came the wolf and saw the little pig in his fine house of sticks. He knocked on the door. 'Little pig, little pig, let me come in.'

The little pig answered, 'No, no, by the hair of my chinny chin chin, I will not let you in.'

And the wolf replied, 'Then I'll huff and I'll puff and I'll blow your house in.' So he huffed and he puffed and he puffed and he huffed, and at last he blew the house in. Then he ate up the second little pig.

The third little pig met a man with a load of bricks. 'Please, man,' he said, 'will you give me that load of bricks?' The man set down the bricks and the little pig built himself a fine house with them.

Along came the wolf and saw the little pig in his fine house of bricks. He knocked on the door. 'Little pig, little pig, let me come in.'

The little pig answered, 'No, no, by the hair of my chinny chin chin, I will not let you in.'

And the wolf replied, 'Then I'll huff and I'll puff and I'll blow your house in.' So he huffed and he puffed, and he puffed and he huffed, and he huffed and he puffed. But he could not blow the house in.

Now the wolf had to think of another way to catch the little pig. He tapped on the window. 'Little pig,' he said, 'Farmer Smith's field is full of turnips. Be ready at six o'clock tomorrow morning and we can go there together.'

The little pig knew that the wolf meant to eat him, so he got up at *five* o'clock the next morning and went to Farmer Smith's field alone. By the time the wolf arrived at six o'clock, the little pig was back at home eating his breakfast. 'Little pig, are you ready?' asked the wolf.

'Ready!' replied the little pig. 'Why, I have been and come back again with a fine potful of turnips for my dinner.'

The wolf was very cross, but he was soon back at the little pig's house with another plan. 'Little pig,' he said, 'there is an apple tree in Merry Garden loaded with apples. Be ready at five o'clock tomorrow morning and we can go there together.'

Next morning the little pig got up at *four* o'clock and went to Merry Garden alone. It was a long walk and he was still picking apples when the wolf arrived.

'These are very good apples, wolf,' said the little pig. 'Try one for yourself.'

He picked an apple and threw it as far as he could, right to the end of Merry Garden. While the wolf was fetching the apple, the little pig climbed down the tree and scampered home as fast as he could.

Now the wolf was really angry, but by the following day he had thought up another plan. 'Little pig,' he said, 'there is a fair at Shanklin this afternoon. Be ready at three o'clock and we can go there together.'

At *two* o'clock the little pig walked up the hill to Shanklin and bought himself a butter churn at the fair. But on his way home he saw the wolf coming up the hill. The little pig did not know what to do, so he climbed into the butter churn to hide. As soon as he was inside, the butter churn fell over and rolled all the way down the hill, right past the wolf. The wolf was so terrified that he ran home and did not go to the fair at all. In the evening he went to the little pig's house.

'Where were you this afternoon?' asked

the little pig.

'This horrible great thing came rolling down
the hill straight at me,' said the wolf. 'I was so
scared I ran home.'

'It was me who scared you then,' said the little pig laughing. 'That horrible great thing rolling down the hill was only me hiding in the butter churn I bought at the fair.'

The wolf was so furious at this that he leapt onto the roof. 'I'm coming down the chimney to eat you up!' he roared.

As soon as the little pig heard the wolf on the roof, he built a great blazing fire and set a huge pot of water to boil on it. When the wolf came roaring down the chimney, the little pig took the lid off the pot. The wolf fell in and was boiled alive, and the little pig ate him for supper.

THE FROG PRINCE

There was once a princess who lived in a magnificent castle. Her rooms were piled high with jewels and finery, but of all her splendid possessions, her favorite was a simple gold ball. One day she threw the ball high in the air and it fell into a pond so deep she could not see the bottom. She sat down and wept.

'I would give anything to get back my beautiful golden ball,' she sobbed. 'My clothes, my jewels, all my precious things.'

Just then a large green frog hopped out of the pond. 'What would I want with clothes and jewels and precious things?' it croaked.

'Go away, you nasty wet creature!' shrieked the princess. 'You can't get my ball back.'

'There you are wrong,' croaked the frog. 'Give me what I want and I will get your ball.'

'What do you want?' asked the princess.

'Take me home with you and let me live with you. Let me eat from your golden plate and sleep in your silken bed,' answered the frog.

The princess shuddered at the thought, but she agreed nevertheless. 'Do you promise?' asked the frog.

'Of course,' said the princess. 'But do hurry!'

The frog dived down into the depths of the pool, and soon it emerged carrying the gold ball. The princess snatched it and ran off towards the castle. 'What about your promise?' called the frog, but the princess ran on without turning round.

That night the princess was eating her supper with the king and queen when something came pattering up the stairs and tapped on the door. Everyone heard the words it spoke:

'Proud princess,
Bar not the door.
Remember your promise,
I ask no more.'

The princess opened
the door and saw the
frog gazing up at her.
She slammed the door
and ran back to the
table. In a moment the
tap came again, and
the voice croaked:

'Proud princess,
Bar not the door.
Remember your promise,
I ask no more.'

Again the princess
opened the door, and
again she shut it in the
frog's face.

When the frog spoke a third time, the king stood up. 'What is the meaning of these words, Daughter?' he asked. When the princess had told her story, the king frowned. 'A promise is a promise, and must be kept,' he said. 'Let your visitor in and do as you have said you will.'

The princess's heart sank, but she opened

the door and the frog hopped up to the table. 'Put me on a stool beside you, Princess, so I may eat at your table,' it said. And the princess had to do as it asked.

'Push your plate a little closer so I may share your supper.' The princess did this and the frog ate. The princess touched nothing. 'Now I am tired,' croaked the frog. 'Take me to your silken bed.'

The princess began to cry, but the king said again, 'A promise is a promise and must be kept.' The sobbing princess picked up the frog and carried it to her bedroom. She set it down in the farthest corner and slipped into bed.

Soon she heard a pattering on the floor and the familiar croaking voice. 'A frog needs sleep the same as a princess,' it said. 'Put me on your silken pillow so I may share your bed.'

The princess did as the frog asked. Then she turned over and cried herself to sleep.

In the morning, when she awoke, she was surprised to see a handsome prince standing beside her bed. 'I was bewitched,' he said, 'and doomed to stay in the shape of a frog until a princess let me come into her home, and eat from her plate, and sleep in her bed.'

The princess remembered how rude she had been to the frog and she felt ashamed. But she and the prince were soon married, and they lived happily for many years.

THE SULTAN'S DAUGHTER

There was once a sultan whose daughter
was so beautiful that every young man in the
kingdom wanted to marry her. But the sultan
did not want his daughter to marry just
anyone. 'He who wishes to marry the Princess
Parizade must first pass a test,' he declared. 'I
shall hide in my garden in three different
places, and anyone who can find me shall have
my daughter for his wife.'

'Easy as winking,' said a fine young prince
who was sure he deserved to win the Princess
Parizade. To begin the test the sultan took the
prince into the garden. The air was heavy with
the scent of flowers. 'A magnificent garden you
have here,' said the prince turning to his host,
but the sultan had already vanished.

The prince walked down the avenues, through the rose arbor and in and out of the summer-house, looking everywhere for the sultan. Finally he sat down by the fish pond. He gazed gloomily at the gold and silver fish darting about the pond, and then he noticed that one particularly large gold fish was wearing a purple turban. The sultan had changed himself into a fish!

'Just as I said,' murmured the prince. 'Easy as winking.' He fetched a net and scooped out the fish with the purple turban. And there stood the sultan, brushing the water out of his eyes.

'That's once,' said the sultan. 'Two more to go,' he added and disappeared. The prince walked round the garden, looking in all the expected places and all the unexpected places to find the sultan. But when night came and he still had not found him, the young prince had to go away disappointed.

The next person to arrive was a rich merchant's son. 'Simple as breathing,' he said

when he saw the sultan's garden. He walked
down the avenues, through the rose arbor, in
and out of the summer-house and round the
fish pond, where he quickly found the fish with
the turban.

'That's once,' said the sultan when he had stopped being a fish. 'Two more to go,' he added and disappeared.

The merchant's son walked round the garden, looking in all the expected places and all the unexpected places, but no sultan could he find. Eventually, tired and hungry, he sat down under a large pear tree. One of the pears was bigger than the rest and it gleamed golden in the evening sun. The merchant's son picked the large gold pear and was about to take a bite out of it when the pear vanished and the sultan stood before him.

'Don't you dare bite me, boy!' he shouted. 'That's twice,' he added. 'One more to go.'

The merchant's son walked round the garden, searching and searching, but he could not find the sultan. Night began to fall and soon it was quite dark. The merchant's son sighed and went away disappointed.

The third person to attempt the test was the young man who looked after the sultan's goats. He had never been into the palace before, and as he entered the throne room he looked about him in wonder. He gazed at the gilded pillars and the embroidered carpets. Then he looked up at the domed roof decorated with moon and

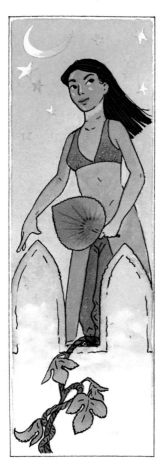

stars. A balcony ran round the foot of the dome, and as he stared the goatherd caught sight of a face peering through the balcony. He recognised the Princess Parizade and he smiled at her. The princess liked the look of the goatherd and she smiled back.

'Stop staring at the ceiling, boy!' roared the sultan, who did not know that his daughter was behind the balcony. 'Let us get on with the test.'

When the goatherd saw the sultan's garden, with all its winding paths and hidden corners, his heart sank. 'It's impossible!' he exclaimed.

But the sultan had already vanished. The goatherd walked down the avenues, through the rose arbor, in and out of the summer-house and round the fish pond, where he quickly found the fish with the turban.

'That's once,' said the sultan. 'Two more to go.' And he disappeared.

The goatherd walked on, looking in all the expected places and all the unexpected places. He soon found the golden pear which was larger than all the rest.

'That's twice!' shouted the sultan. 'One more to go.'

The goatherd walked round and round the garden, searching and searching for the sultan. Night was beginning to fall and soon it was quite dark. 'I do wish I could win the princess,' sighed the goatherd, and he sat down under a large rosebush by the summer-house.

'Though I don't deserve her at all, since I'm only a poor goatherd.'

'A goatherd will do for me,' said the princess, who had been hiding in the summer-house. She looked so lovely that the goatherd

reached up and plucked a rose to give to her. Immediately the rose vanished and the sultan appeared.

'How did you guess?' he roared. 'That rose was just like all the rest!'

The princess and the goatherd never told the sultan that it was only by the merest chance that the goatherd had picked that particular rose. And the sultan gave away his daughter with a happy heart because he was sure he had chosen the right husband for her. The goatherd may not have been the noblest or richest young man in the kingdom, but he was certainly the cleverest. Of that the sultan was sure.

THE ENORMOUS TURNIP

In a small country not far away lived two brothers. One was a rich banker who spent all his time eating and drinking. The other was a poor farmer who worked hard all year round and never made a penny.

One spring the poor farmer planted a row of turnips. After a few weeks the seeds put up leaves and the turnips began to swell. The farmer noticed that one turnip was much larger than the rest. He watched it grow and grow and grow until by the end of the summer it was as large as a haystack.

'That turnip is far too large for two people to eat,' the farmer said to his wife. 'I think I shall give it to the king instead.' Two oxen dragged the enormous turnip out of the ground.

Then the farmer and his wife pushed and shoved and heaved the turnip into the ox-cart, and the farmer drove it to the king's palace.

The king and his court were delighted with the enormous turnip. 'You must be a man of extraordinary luck to grow such a fine turnip,' the king said to the farmer.

'To tell you the truth, Your Majesty,' replied the farmer, 'this is the first piece of luck to come my way. I have worked hard every day of my life and never made a penny. My brother the banker has never done a day's work, and he is ten times richer than me.'

'Now your luck has changed!' declared the king. 'In return for your generous gift, I shall give you houses and lands and cows and gold which will make you ten times richer than your brother.' And the farmer went home a very happy man.

When the rich banker heard of his brother's luck, he was filled with envy. 'If the king can give such wealth in return for a mere turnip,' he thought to himself, 'what will he give in return for something really precious?' The banker filled a chest with his most costly treasures, and immediately took it to the palace. The king received the chest in silence. The banker bowed.

'I thank you for your gift,' said the king. 'And in return I shall give you my most precious possession.'

The banker's eyes widened with greed. Then, to his horror, he saw the courtiers wheeling out the king's most precious possession – his brother's enormous turnip! There was nothing for the banker to do but thank the king and take the turnip home to his wife, who was not at all pleased.